An Ant's Day Off

by Bonny Becker

illustrated by Nina Laden

SIMON & SCHUSTER BOOKS FOR YOUNG READERS
New York   London   Toronto   Sydney   Singapore

In memory of my mother and father, who gave me time to look at the sky —B. B.

For my brother, David, who could use a day off or two —N. L.

SIMON & SCHUSTER BOOKS FOR YOUNG READERS
An imprint of Simon & Schuster Children's Publishing Division
1230 Avenue of the Americas, New York, New York 10020

Book design by Paula Winicur
The text for this book is set in Vendetta Medium.
The illustrations are rendered in pastels.
Manufactured in China

2 4 6 8 10 9 7 5 3 1

Library of Congress Cataloging-in-Publication Data
Becker, Bonny.
An ant's day off / by Bonny Becker; illustrations by Nina Laden.—1st ed.
p. cm.
Summary: Having taken a day off from his job moving sand inside the nest, Bart the ant
ventures into the outside world, meets other animals, and experiences both danger and fun.
ISBN 0-689-82274-X
[1. Ants—Fiction. 2. Animals—Fiction.] I. Laden, Nina, ill. II. Title.

PZ7.B3814 An 2001
[E]—dc21
99-022598

"I'm taking the day off," said Bart. "I'm tired of working."

"No ant has ever taken the day off," his friend Floyd reminded him, nervously glancing about. "Never ever in the history of antdom."

Bart and Floyd were sand ants. They spent their days under the ground working all the time. They had never seen the sky or felt the rain.

But this morning, as Bart toiled about the mound of sand he was to move
from Tunnel 929B to Tunnel 49A, he glanced up. High above was a glimmer of blue,
far and away, and it called to him, "Come, little ant. Come out and play."

"You must work and work and work some more," Floyd said, seeing the wild gleam
in Bart's eye. "Happiness is a finished chore!"

But it was too late. Bart threw down his load of sand and began to climb.

"Don't!" cried Floyd. "They'll never let you back in!"

Up and up Bart scrambled until his head popped out into a
bright spring day. He nearly fainted with the shock of it all.
The sky was too high to imagine an end to it. A breeze tugged at his
antennae and the sun felt golden warm on his head.

"Get a move on!" barked a stern ant guarding the nest. "Food patrol
is over there." Bart hurried down the mound to join the line.

All the other ants kept their eyes straight ahead and their noses
to the ground as they marched toward the remains of a giant bagel,
but Bart saw an opening in the grass and scurried away.

He came to a broad river.

"Row," said a voice.

"Row," said another voice.

Bart peered around the edge of a water iris. He saw two frogs.

"Gently down the stream," said one frog.

"Merrily, merrily, merrily, merrily," said the other frog.

And together they croaked, "Life is but a dream."

Bart hopped onto a leaf lying near the water's edge
and pushed himself out into the stream.

"Hello!" he cried to the frogs.

Then, to his horror, the larger frog snapped
a fly into its mouth.

The smaller frog eyed Bart hungrily.

The frog's
tongue flicked
out, but just then
the current picked
up, and Bart floated
out of reach.
The little frog settled
back with a blink.
"Row," he croaked.
"Row," croaked the big frog.
Inside his head, Bart heard
a tiny voice. It sounded just like Floyd.
"Always work, never rest. You see what comes
of idleness," the Floyd voice said.
"Perhaps I should go back to the nest," Bart thought.
Suddenly, his leaf caught on a branch and spun to a stop.

Bart scrambled to the shore.

A tall dandelion stood in his way. Maybe he would see just a bit more of the world before he went back.

The petals were soft. The sun was warm.
For the first time in his life, Bart wasn't
doing anything.

"Don't you feel bad," the Floyd voice said,
"lying here, lazy and useless, while your fellow ants
struggle below?"

"I guess I do," Bart thought. But it was very pleasant just the same.

He yawned and closed his eyes. Was this a nap?
He'd heard tales of such things back in the nest.

The air beat against him in gentle, tickling waves.

"Hmmmmm," Bart murmured. "Ahhhhhhh."

He rolled over.

Hovering above him was a huge honeybee brimming with pollen. Down she came, landing right on top of him.

"Help!" he squawked.

The bee busily gathered her pollen, then took off—taking Bart with her!

She flew up and down and up and down.

Bart could see sky and field and sky and field.

"AHHHH—!"

A sneeze tickled at his nose.

"AHHHHCHOOOOO!"

Bart fell down, down, down and landed with a *WHUMP!* on another dandelion.

He scrambled to his feet.

"I'm alive," he cried. "And I'm probably the only sand ant ever in the history of antdom to fly."

Bart didn't notice the dark clouds in the sky.

Plop. Plop. Plippity, plop, plop, plop!

Bart looked up. His first-ever rain!

SPLOSH! SPLOSH! Raindrops burst upon him.

The dandelion swayed. Bart slipped off into a puddle and came up gasping. He had to get back to the nest!

"They'll never let you back in." Floyd's words came rushing back. "Get a move on! Never stop. Never tarry. An ant who wastes time will never marry!"

They all came back to him, the words every ant heard from the day he was hatched.

He staggered up to the entrance of the nest.
There at the top stood the guard ant.

Bart realized with a horrible start that he carried nothing—
no lace bug wing, no bagel crumb, not even a grain of sand.
Nothing useful!

"Halt!" cried the guard. "Who goes there?"

"It's me," stammered Bart. "Bart, the sand ant."

"Sand ant? What are you doing out here?"

Wild lies flashed through Bart's head. Maybe he could say
he was kidnapped by earthworms. Or that he was blind.
"I took a day off," Bart whispered. "I'm not doing anything.
I'm being totally and completely useless.
I floated down a stream, I almost took a nap,
and I flew on a bee . . . but that was mostly by mistake."
"A day off?" said the guard. "You took the day off?"
Bart nodded miserably.

The guard paused and then said quietly, "I took a day off once, long ago."
"You did?" breathed Bart.
"Don't tell anyone," snapped the guard. "Not a peep,
never a word. Still, if you'll pick up that moth wing and make it snappy,
I'll let you back in."
"Always bring back a bit of something," muttered the guard,
as Bart slipped past. "That's what the others do."
"Others?" Bart asked.
"Sometimes," the guard said softly.
"Well, sometimes an ant just needs to look at the sky, now doesn't he?"
Then he frowned and turned away.

Bart hurried to Tunnel 929B.

Floyd had cleared away his mound of sand and Bart's, too.

"I'll do twice as much tomorrow," Bart promised.

"Tell me about your day off," Floyd whispered. "Tell me everything."

And Bart did. Once, twice, again and again, all through the long summer, Bart told Floyd about sun and frogs and rain.